Prairie Primer
A to Z

by Caroline Stutson

illustrated by Susan Condie Lamb

Dutton Children's Books · New York

Text copyright © 1996 by Caroline Stutson   Illustrations copyright © 1996 by Susan Condie Lamb   All rights reserved.

Library of Congress Cataloging-in-Publication Data
Stutson, Caroline. Prairie primer / by Caroline Stutson; illustrated by Susan Condie Lamb.—1st ed. p. cm.
Summary: Life on the prairie is depicted in this rhyming alphabet book.   ISBN 0-525-45163-3
[1. Frontier and pioneer life—Fiction. 2. Stories in rhyme. 3. Alphabet.] I. Lamb, Susan Condie, ill. II. Title.
PZ8.3.S925Pr 1996   [E]—dc20   95-45811 CIP AC

Published in the United States 1996 by Dutton Children's Books,
a division of Penguin Books USA Inc.
375 Hudson Street, New York, New York 10014

Designed by Semadar Megged   Printed in Hong Kong   First Edition
10 9 8 7 6 5 4 3 2 1

To Candace, with love
With special thanks to the Littleton Historical Museum

C.S.

To Chris, Charlie, and Ella—
for believing that painted pies are just as yummy

S.C.L.

A the Alphabet I'll learn

B for Butter in the churn

C so Cozy by the stove

D we're rolling out the Dough

E brown Eggs I mustn't drop

F the Firewood we chop

G for greedy Guinea hens

H the House that calls us in

"Coming! Coming!" we all sing,
on the porch for one last swing.

I two Irons growing hot, breakfast porridge in the pot

When the bowls are
cleared away...

J

a game of Jacks we play.

Long black stockings,
high-top shoes,

K

for Knickers and
Kazoos

L

the Lunch pails
packed for school

M

this trifling, stubborn Mule!

 for one bad Nanny goat,
pulling buttons from my coat

O our Oxen in the pen

P there's Piggy out again!

Sunday morning, dressed for church,
down the road we bump and lurch.

 for Quiet much too long

R the rafters Ring with song!

Fabric scraps of green
and purple,

S

for ladies' Sewing circle

Teetotum spins for fun

U Umbrella shades the sun

Pedals flying, racing speed,

V

a blue Velocipede!

Carved by Papa...
bright and big,

W

new Whirligig

Count the crosses Sister's stitched...
her first sampler made with **X**

Y another Year for me
with birthday cake beneath the tree

Z the days Zipped by so fast
but now it's time for bed at last...
now it's time for bed at last.